Corky Cub's Crazy Caps

by Barbara deRubertis • illustrated by R.W. Alley

THE KANE PRESS / NEW YORK

Alpha Betty's Class

Dilly Dog

Alexander Anteater

Bobby Baboon

STAR of the BOOK

Corky Cub

Hanna Hippo

Eddie Elephant

Frances Frog

Gertie Gorilla

Lana Llama

Izzy Impala

Jeremy Jackrabbit

Kylie Kangaroo

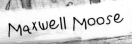

Maxwell Moose

Nina Nandu

Oliver Otter

Polly Porcupine

Quentin Quokka

Rosie Raccoon

Sammy Skunk

Tessa Tiger

Umma Ungka

Victor Vicuna

Walter Warthog

Xavier Ox

Yoko Yak

Zachary Zebra

Alpha Betty

Library of Congress Cataloging-in-Publication Data

deRubertis, Barbara.
Corky Cub's crazy caps / by Barbara deRubertis ; illustrated by R.W. Alley.
    p. cm. — (Animal Antics A to Z)
Summary: Corky Cub is sad when Connie Cougar moves away, so teacher Alpha Betty
suggests a project to help him make new friends.
ISBN 978-1-57565-306-8 (lib. bdg. : alk. paper) — ISBN 978-1-57565-302-0 (pbk. : alk. paper)
[1. Bears—Fiction. 2. Hats—Fiction. 3. Friendship—Fiction 4. Clubs—Fiction. 5. Animals—
Fiction. 6. Humorous stories. 7. Alphabet.] I. Alley, R. W. (Robert W.), ill. II. Title.
PZ7.D4475Ck 2010
    [E]—dc22   2009024484

10 9 8 7 6 5 4 3 2 1

First published in the United States of America
in 2010 by Kane Press, Inc.
Printed in Hong Kong
Reinforced Library Binding by Muscle Bound Bindery,
Minneapolis, MN

Series Editor: Juliana Hanford
Book Design: Edward Miller

Animal Antics A to Z is a trademark of Kane Press, Inc.

www.kanepress.com

Corky Cub played with Connie Cougar every day after school.

They were best friends. Pals. Chums.

And they always wore matching caps.

Corky and Connie played catch.

They colored with crayons.

And they made
chocolate chip cookies.

But most of all, they liked
adding crazy creations to
their matching caps!

One day, Connie told Corky she had
bad news. VERY bad news.

Corky held his breath.

Connie sniffed. She hiccupped.
And then she continued.
"I'm moving awaaaaaaay!"

"Oh, NO!" said Corky.
"You're my best chum!"

The two friends were much too sad
to eat their chocolate chip cookies.

Too soon, moving day came.

Corky and Connie wore their
favorite caps.

They said good-bye.

And they both cried as
Connie's car drove away.

Corky Cub was so lonely.

He couldn't play catch.
And he did NOT want to color pictures.
OR make chocolate chip cookies.

"Call some other chums," said Mama.

"I can't. I don't have any other chums,"
said Corky.

"Make some new chums," said Papa.

"I can't. I don't know how to make new chums," said Corky.

Corky climbed up the stairs.
And he crawled into bed.

The next day, Corky was late for school.
His teacher, Alpha Betty, asked Corky why
he looked so sad.

"My only chum moved away," said Corky.

"That IS a problem," said Alpha Betty.
"Let's put on our thinking caps."

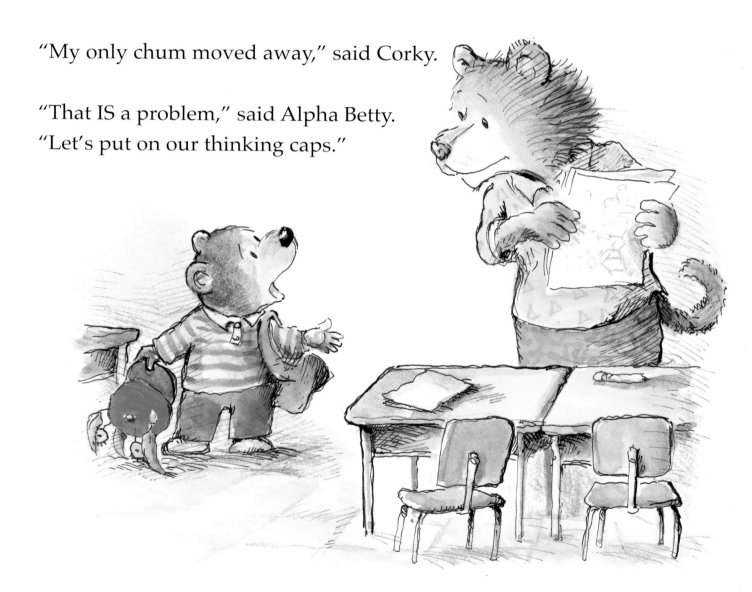

Then she chuckled. "Oh! CAPS!
That has given me an idea.
Create a new cap, Corky.
A friend-making cap!

Wear your new cap tomorrow.
And wear your most cheerful smile!"

That night Corky created a friend-making cap.
He hoped it would give him courage.

Mama and Papa helped.

They cut out colorful patches.

They clipped on pins.

They sewed on cool buttons.

And they put a crazy pinwheel on top!

Corky wore his new cap as he walked to school the next day. And he practiced smiling.

Casey Crow cawed,
"Colorful cap, Corky!"

Carrie Cat called,
"Cute cap, Corky!"

And Calvin Camel caught
Corky's arm. "COOL cap,
dude!" said Calvin.

Corky walked into school wearing his most
cheerful smile. Alpha Betty smiled, too.

In a brave voice, Corky called out,
"Hi, everybody!"

Corky's classmates all looked up.
They saw Corky's cap.

Then they went crazy! They wanted to know how he made it.

"Bring a cap tomorrow," said Corky. "I can help you make cool caps, too!"

The next day, Corky carried two big
sacks to school. He was so excited!

In one sack were colorful patches.
Clip-on pins. Cool buttons.
And crazy pinwheels.

In the other sack was a carton of
Corky's tasty chocolate chip cookies.

Corky's class made very creative caps.
Then they ate the tasty chocolate chip cookies.

Everyone thanked Corky Cub.
And Corky said, "You're welcome!"
Then he smiled without even trying.

"May we wear our crazy caps every Friday?" the class asked their teacher.

"We could have a Crazy Cap Club!" said Corky.

"What a cool idea!" said Alpha Betty.

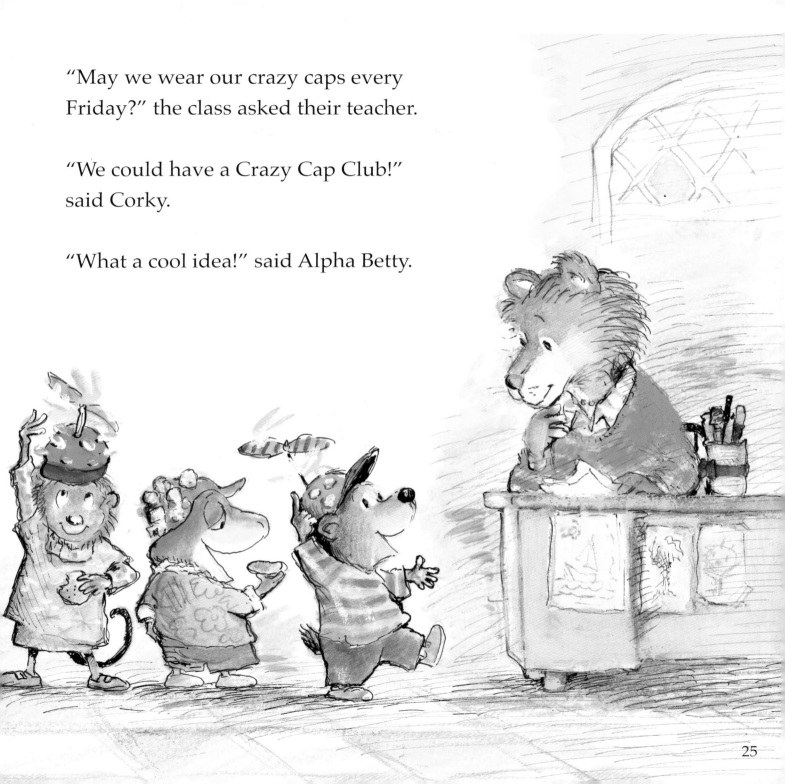

So the children started having Crazy
Cap Club meetings every Friday.

They wore their crazy caps.

They made chocolate chip cookies.

And Corky had more chums than he could count!

Corky still missed Connie Cougar, of course.
So he sent her a COOL package.

"Dear Connie," he wrote on the card.
"Here's a picture of me in my new crazy cap.
I made a crazy cap for you, too!

Chums Forever,
Corky Cub"

Connie loved her crazy cap.
She quickly wrote back to Corky.

"Thank you, Corky!
You're still my best chum.
And guess what!
I can come to visit you this summer!"

Corky Cub and his old chum had a great visit.

And Corky and his new chums invited Connie to join their club!

Everyone in the Crazy Cap Club
had a terrific time that summer . . .

and for many summers after!

FUN FACTS

- Home: North America, usually in forests
- Weight: About 200 pounds—but some grow to over 800 pounds!
- Favorite foods: Berries, roots, and some animals. And don't leave food out at a campsite. Bears will find it and eat it!
- Baby bears: When black bear cubs are born, they are nearly hairless. And their eyes stay closed for about a month.
- **Did You Know?** Black bears are excellent tree-climbers!

LOOK BACK

Learning to identify letter sounds (phonemes) at the beginning, middle, and end of words is called "phonemic awareness."

You'll need your "thinking cap" for this activity!

- The word *cub* <u>begins</u> with the *c* sound. Listen to the words on pages 10–11 being read again. When you hear a word that begins with the *c* sound, lift up your cap and say the word!
- The word *sack* <u>ends</u> with the *ck* sound. Listen to the words in the box being read. When you hear a word that <u>ends</u> with the *ck* sound, lift your cap and say the word!

> back came cut crack card Jack
> come pack tack crazy rack quack

- **JUST FOR FUN**: Decorate *your* cap!

TRY THIS!

Put the cookies in the cookie jars!

Set three bowls or containers in a row for "cookie jars." Draw 12 cookies on a piece of paper. You can color and decorate the cookies if you like! Then cut them out.

- Listen carefully as each word in the word bank below is slowly read aloud. If the word <u>begins</u> with the *c* sound, put a cookie in the first jar.
- If the word has the *c* sound in the <u>middle</u>, put a cookie in the middle jar.
- If a word has the *ck* sound at the <u>end</u>, put a cookie in the third jar.

> cub tack hiccup car color sack
> cool practice trick come stick cap